In memory of Our Doris, my fantastic mum,
and for Jane, wonderful mother of our children
—A.B.

First published in Great Britain by Doubleday, a division of Transworld Publishers, 2005
Printed in Singapore
Designed by Ian Butterworth
First American edition, 2005
1 3 5 7 9 10 8 6 4 2

Library of Congress Cataloging-in-Publication Data
Browne, Anthony, date.
My mom / Anthony Browne.— 1st American ed.
p. cm.
Summary: A child describes the many wonderful things about "my mom," who can make anything grow, roar like a lion, and be as comfy as an armchair.
ISBN-13: 978-0-374-35098-7
ISBN-10: 0-374-35098-1
[1. Mothers—Fiction. 2. Mother and child—Fiction.] I. Title.
PZ7.B81276My 2005
[E]—dc22
2004047173

My Mom

Anthony Browne

FARRAR STRAUS GIROUX
New York

She's nice, my mom.

My mom's a fantastic cook,

and a brilliant juggler.

She's a great painter,

and the STRONGEST
woman in the world!

She’s really nice, my mom.

My mom's a magic gardener;
she can make ANYTHING grow.

And she's a good fairy;
when I'm sad she can make me happy.

She can sing like an angel,

and roar like a lion.

She's really, REALLY nice, my mom.

My mom's as beautiful as a butterfly,

and as comfy
as an
armchair.

She’s as soft as a kitten,

and as tough as a rhino.

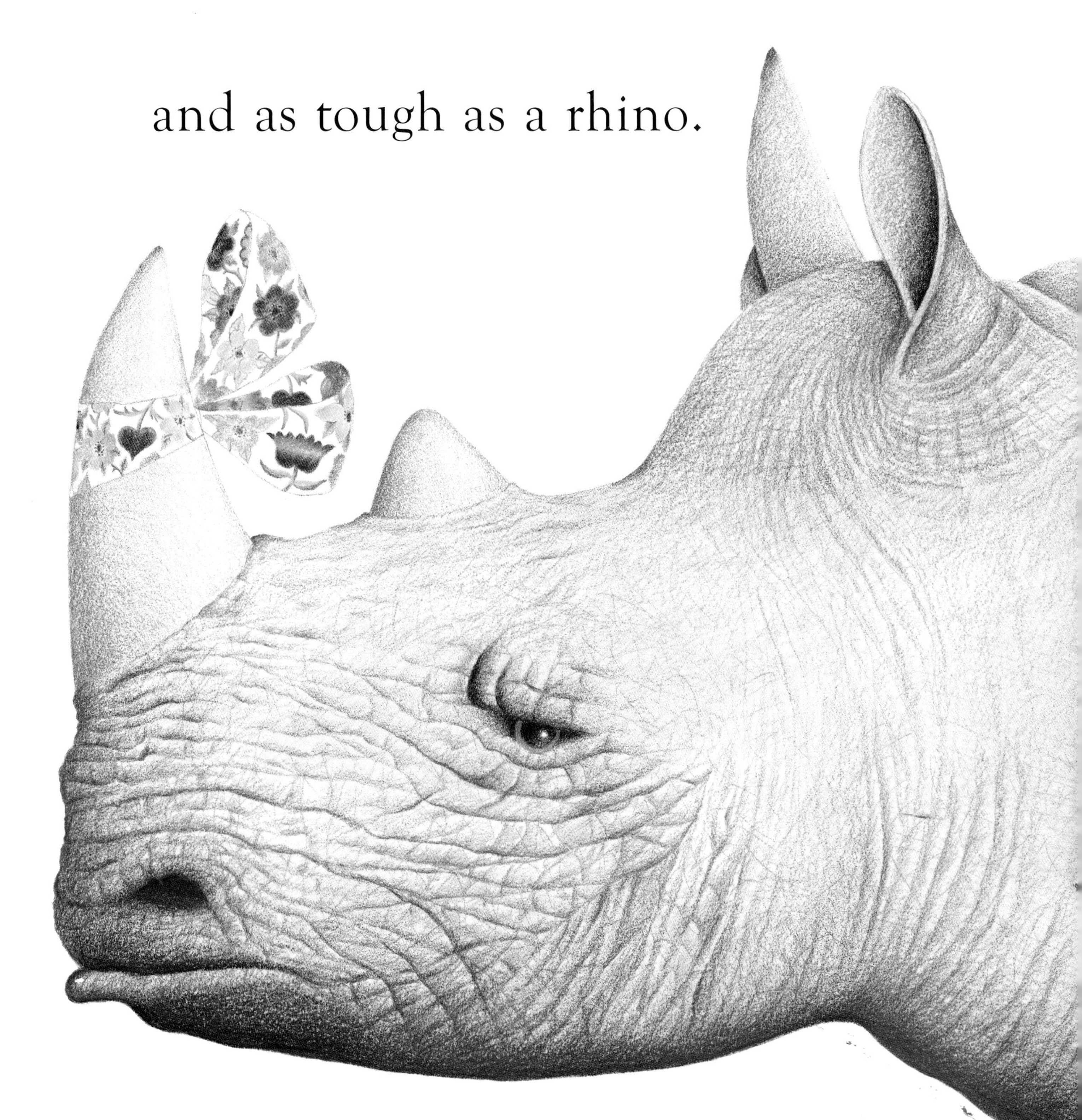

She's really, REALLY,
REALLY nice, my mom.

My mom could be a dancer,

or an astronaut.

She could be a film star,

or the big boss. But she's MY mom.

She's a SUPERMOM!

And she makes me laugh. A lot.

I love my mom.

And you know what?

SHE LOVES ME!

(And she always will.)